CAROLYN LESSER

DIG HOLE, SOFT MOLE

ILLUSTRATED BY LAURA REGAN

Harcourt Brace & Company

SAN DIEGO   NEW YORK   LONDON

With appreciation to my mother, Anita Schmidt,
who loved the sound of these words. —C. L.

Library of Congress Cataloging-in-Publication Data
Lesser, Carolyn.
Dig hole, soft mole/Carolyn Lesser;
illustrated by Laura Regan.—1st ed.
p.   cm.
Summary: A mole travels underground and
underwater, exploring marsh and pond.
ISBN 0-15-223491-8
1. Moles (Animals)—Juvenile fiction.
[1. Moles (Animals)—Fiction.]
I. Regan, Laura, ill.   II. Title.
PZ10.3.L553Di   1996
[E]—dc20   95-11697

First edition
A B C D E

Printed in Singapore

The illustrations in this book were done in oil and gouache on illustration board.
The display type was set in Blackfriar and the text type was set in Goudy by
Harcourt Brace & Company Photocomposition Center, San Diego, California.
Color separations by Bright Arts, Ltd., Singapore
Printed and bound by Tien Wah Press, Singapore
This book was printed with soya-based inks on Leykam recycled paper,
which contains more than 20 percent postconsumer waste and has
a total recycled content of at least 50 percent.
Production supervision by Warren Wallerstein and Ginger Boyer
Designed by Lori J. McThomas

For Nancy Ryan,
mountain woman, teacher, and friend.
Thank you for lighting the path.

—C. L.

For Michelle, Matthew, and Luke, with love.

—L. R.

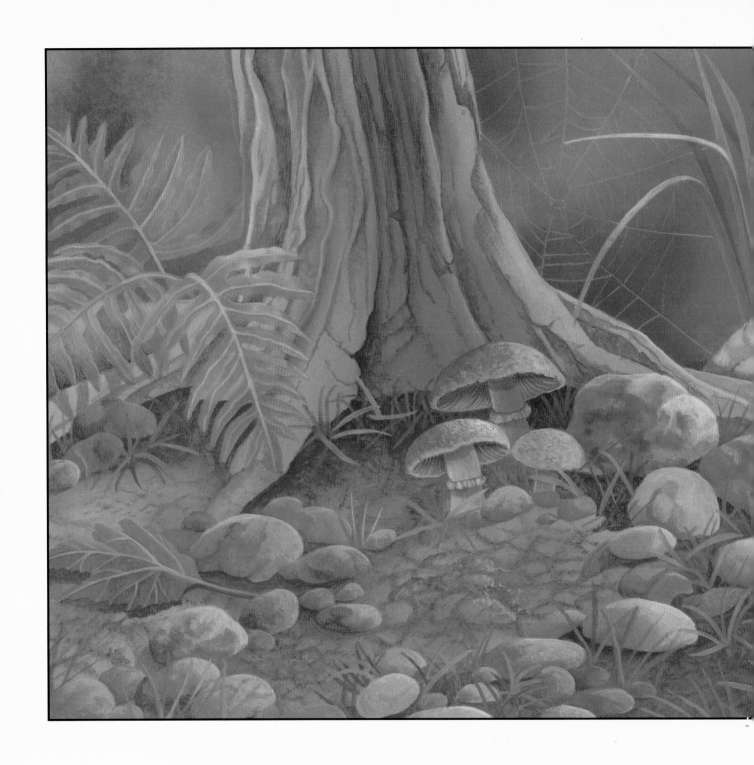

Dig hole, soft mole,

In woodsy jumble, topsoil crumble.

Crickets hop, twigs pop.

Centipedes slink under leaves.

Starry nose feels and goes.
Hidden ears hear wood frog toes.

Pebbly paws, left, right.
Underground is dark as night.

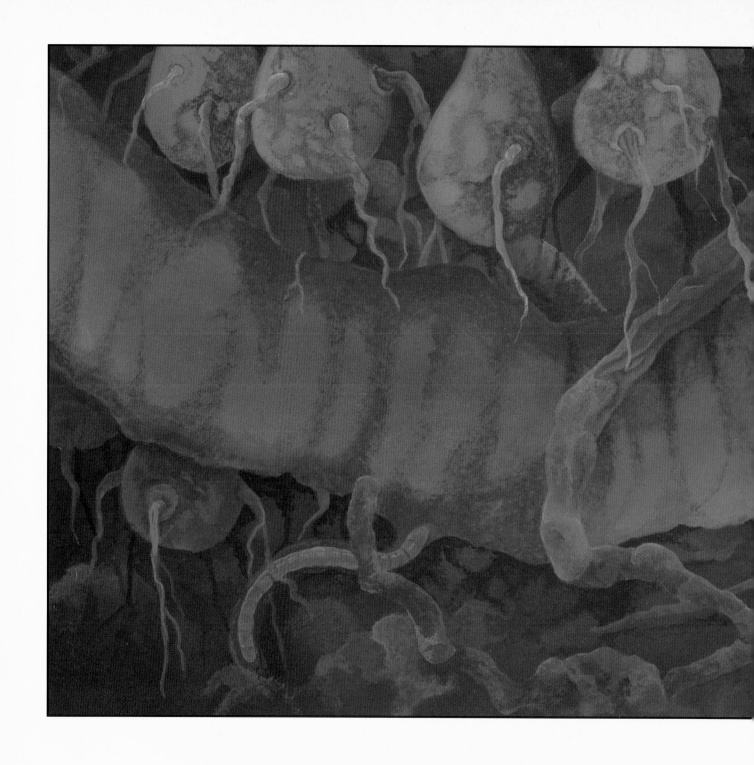

Nestled deep, bulbs sleep.
Bugs creep, creep deep.

Snakes and worms detour, squirm,
'Round rocks and stones, earthy bones.

To turn about, a somersault,
Fur back and forth, south or north.

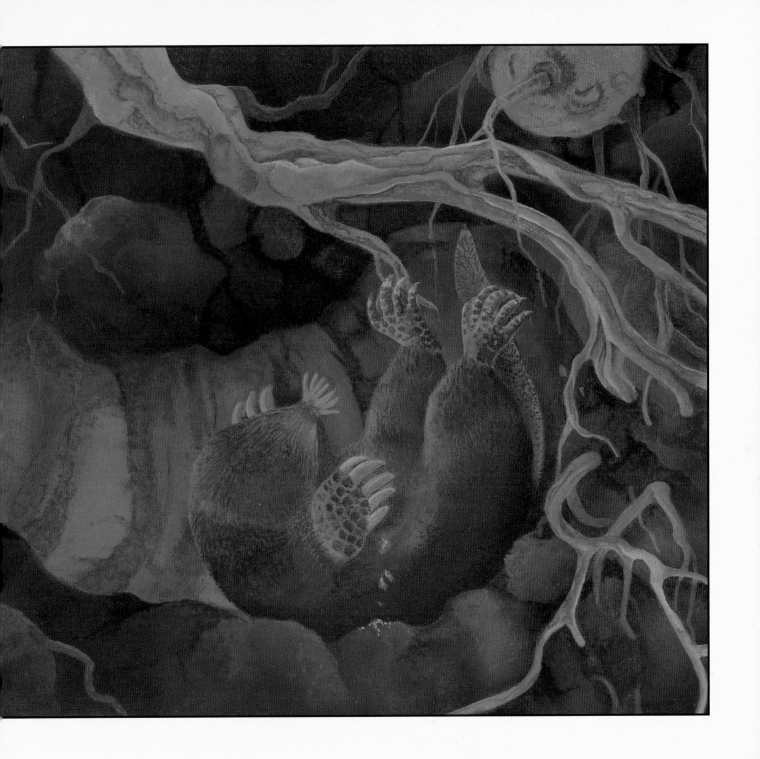

Deeper down, craggy chunks.
Roots slink over bedrock hunks.

Scoop and scrabble, burrow through,

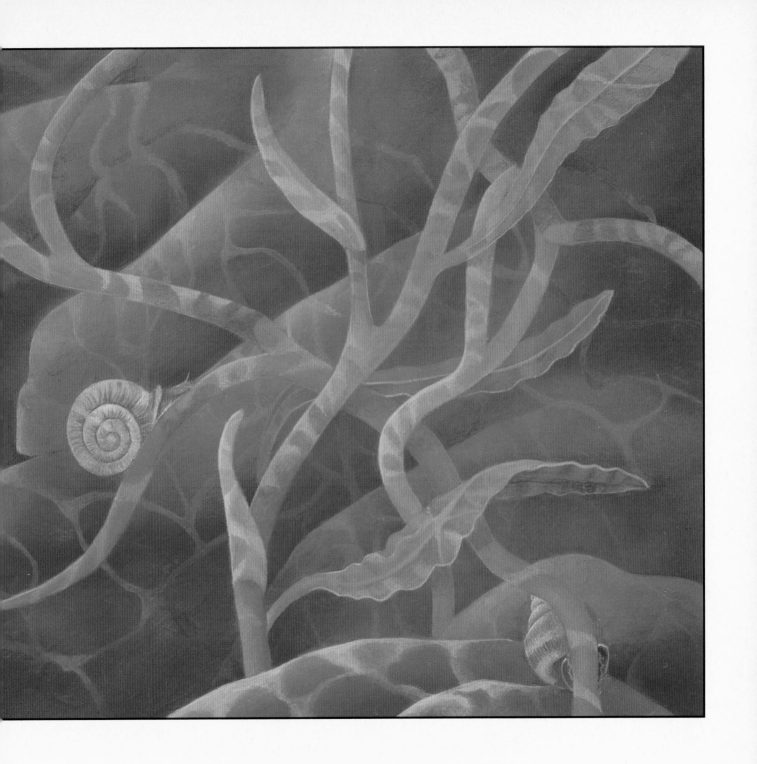

Tunnel into deepest blue.

Pulling feet, sculling tail,
Furry boat without a sail.

Hungry, prowling, dinner wish,
Dive and feel for snails and fish.

Mole strokes up to shimmery top.

Cranes prance a dance, leap and hop.

Paddle past twiggy domes,

Cozy clumps, muskrat homes.

Cattails, bulrushes swerve and sway.

Blackbirds, dragonflies lift away.

Maple branch holds wood duck feet.

Teal speed by, trim and neat.

Setting sun, rising moon
Open water lily blooms.

Hidden inside, tucked in tight,
Midnight bug snack—snip, snap, bite!

Hush of night in grassy nest,
Starlit owl flies east and west.

From moonlit glade, a thirsty fawn,
On misty pond, a ghostly swan.

Day and night in marsh and pool,
Soil damp, water cool.

Treasures wait in brown or blue,
Star-nosed mole, all for you.

DATE			